THE PARABLE OF
BARTHOLOMEW BEAVER
AND THE
STUPENDOUS SPLASH

In Which the Windy Woods Campers Learn the Biblical Value of Encouragement

By Michael Waite
Illustrated by Sheila Lucas

Encourage each other every day

Hebrews 3:13

Dear Parents: *Read* Bartholomew Beaver *aloud with your family. Talk about the story and how you can encourage each other. Discuss Hebrews 3:13 and memorize it together. The verse will serve as a reminder of the Christian value of encouragement.*

Don't miss these other Camp Windy Woods books and toys!

· Digger's Marvelous Moleberry Patch
· Shelby the Magnificent
· Butterflies for Two

· Daisy Doddlepaws and the Windy Woods Treasure
· Lady Bug Island
· Camp Windy Woods Peel and Play

Bartholomew Beaver hid in the bushes and stared out across the lake at Lady Bug Island. Lucy Goosefeathers and Barnaby Hopthistle had just got their Swimmer's Badges and now they were jumping into the lake off the Big Rope Swing. He watched Lucy swoop out over the water, high, high into the air, laughing and kicking. Then she dropped to the water with a stupendous splash! Bartholomew wanted more than anything to paddle out and join them. But the lake looked so horribly dark and deep.

"Oh, crumbs," he said with a sigh. "I'll never get my Swimmer's Badge. I'd just sink to the bottom and that would be the end of it." He sighed again and kicked a stone off the pathway. "I'll never get to go off the Big Rope Swing. I just know it."

He hid his swim trunks and towel in a stump beside the trail and hurried down to the dock to watch the others.

When he got there, Daisy Doddlepaws and Anthony Dormouse were perched at the edge of the dock, looking rather trembly and pale. He gave them each a cookie for extra strength. Then he patted their shoulders with towels to keep them warm.

"It's your turn next, Bartholomew," said Uncle Beardsley. "Oh… um…" said Bartholomew, rubbing his nose and coughing a bit. "I think I might be coming down with the snuffles."

Uncle Beardsley blew his whistle, and Daisy and Anthony dove into the water. They popped to the surface and began swimming toward Lady Bug Island.

"Go, Daisy! Go, Anthony!" cried Bartholomew. He jumped up and down on the dock, whirling his arms through the air like a swimmer. "Paddle! Kick! You're almost there!"

He clapped and cheered as they swam all the way out to the Island. Then they scrambled out of the water and ran straight to the Big Rope Swing. Swoosh—through the air they went! Kersplash! They laughed and splashed and waved back at Bartholomew. How he wanted to join them!

"Alrighty, Bartholomew," said Uncle Beardsley. "Time to go suit up. It's your turn."

Bartholomew tried sniffling and coughing a bit more, but Uncle Beardsley didn't seem to notice.

So he shuffled back to Pondwater Cabin and put on his swimming shorts. Then he plopped down on the front walk and sighed.

"What's the use?" he said to himself. "I'll sink right to the bottom. Then everyone will know I can't swim. They'll make fun of me and call me names, and I'll never get to go off the Big Rope Swing."

He sat there for a long time, eating chockle-nut cookies and pudding cakes. But nothing made him feel any better. Just then, he noticed a long rope hanging from Anthony's treehouse, and it gave him an idea.

11

He raked up a big pile of leaves, grabbed
the rope, and climbed on top of a tall stump. Then—
wheeeeee!—he swung high into the air and let go. For a long,
wonderful moment, he seemed to float in the sky. Then, suddenly, he
dropped onto his belly with a soft, leafy splash! It was so much fun that
he jumped up to do another one. Just then, he heard voices coming up
the path.

"Barthoooooolomew!" sang someone.

"Oh, Baaarty-Poo!" called someone else.

He ducked behind a tree and peered down the pathway. In a moment, three of his friends came skipping round the bend. They were dripping wet from the lake, and they were laughing and shoving and squeezing water all over each other.

"Crumbs and double crumbs!" groaned Bartholomew. "They've come to get me for my swimming test. They'll find out I can't swim and call me a Bawl-Beaver. Hopeless. It's all hopeless."

He slipped behind the cabin and scurried off into the woods.

But Bartholomew was not a very speedy beaver and soon he could hear the voices growing closer behind him. No matter which way he turned, he couldn't seem to lose them.

"Oh, Baaaaaarty!" called Daisy Doddlepaws. "Wait for us!"

Suddenly, he found himself trapped against the Frog Pond, with nowhere left to go.

He scrambled onto a mossy log and scuttled across it as fast as he could—but he really couldn't—and before he knew what was happening, the log was going one way and he was going the other, and he hit the water with a giant splash!

"Help! Oh, help!" he cried splashing and spitting out water.

Daisy Doddlepaws dove into the pond and dragged him to shore. He sat slumped against a rock on the bank. Bits of lily pad stuck to his nose and tadpoles wiggled in his ears.

"Oh, Bartholomew!" cried Lucy Goosefeathers, patting him dry with her towel. "We didn't know you couldn't swim!"

"Go ahead," he sniffled miserably. "Make fun. Call me a Bawl-Beaver. I don't care. Won't bother me a bit." And he hid his face in his paws.

"Don't be such a silly-pants!" said Daisy. "We're your friends. We're not going to pick on you."

"Hmf," mumbled Bartholomew.

"Yeah," said Anthony. "We wanted to clap and holler while you got your Swimmy Badge, just like you did for us."

"Then we could all swim out to Lady Bug Island and go off the Big Rope Swing!" added Lucy.

"Except," said Bartholomew, gloomily. "I can't even swim two strokes."

"Oh, yes you can," said Daisy. "You just wait and see!"

Bartholomew followed them down to the lake, and they dressed him up in floaties and flippers and goggles. Then they helped him into the water and set him afloat.

Daisy showed him how to kick his feet. Lucy showed him how to paddle his paws. And Anthony showed him how to squirt water between his teeth. (He was especially good at this).

21

Before long, Bartholomew could paddle back and forth without anyone holding on. After a bit longer, he could swim without flippers or floaties. And after two whole weeks of practice, he could paddle right out into the deep water and back again without anything but his four paws and his tail.

"Hello! Look at me!" he cried, paddling round Uncle Beardsley's boat. "I'm swimming!"

Everyone clapped and cheered, and Bartholomew opened a box of his very best cookies to celebrate.

"Well," said Uncle Beardsley, "Looks to me like you're ready to earn that Swimmer's Badge, Bartholomew!"

Bartholomew suddenly felt very nervous.

"Seems awfully windy today," he said doubtfully. "Looks like rain, too."

"Nonsense!" laughed Uncle Beardsley. "You'll be out to Lady Bug Island before you know it, flying off the Big Rope Swing!"

Bartholomew gazed out at the Big Rope Swing hopefully. It looked like a tremendously long way.

All the campers piled into Uncle Beardsley's canoe and he rowed out to the end of the dock.

"Ready, Bartholomew?" he shouted.

"Well, actually..." Bartholomew began.

Before he could finish, Uncle Beardsley blew his whistle.

Bartholomew pinched his nose and plunged into the water.

The minute he bobbed to the top, he knew it was no use. He was so scared he could barely move. He was just about to turn around and head for shore when, suddenly, he heard a wonderful sound....

"Hooray, Barty!"
"You can do it, Bartholomew!"
"Paddle, Barty! Paddle for all you're worth!"
And at that very moment his whole insides filled up with beavery
courage, and his paws began kicking, and his tail started flapping, and away
he went, splashing through the water faster than he'd ever swum before!

Almost before he knew what was happening, right there in front of him stood Lady Bug Island! Everyone cheered and shouted and jumped all over the happy swimmer. Uncle Beardsley handed him his Badge, and Bartholomew pinned it to his swim shorts proudly.

Then, he ran straight to the Big Rope Swing, with everyone else laughing and chasing after him. He swung far out over the lake—higher than he'd ever dreamed! Then he dropped to the water with the loudest, wettest, most stupendous splash to ever splatter the banks of Lady Bug Island.

EVERYBODY NEEDS A BEAVER BUDDY

An Encouragement Hum
by Lucy Goosefeathers

Oh, the trail is long and the wind is strong
And the ground is oh-so-muddy
If I trip and fall, won't you grab my paw?
'Cause everybody needs a beaver buddy!

Laaa-dee-dum, it's a dream come true,
You for me! Me for you!
Laaa-dee-dum, what a pair, we two!
Everybody needs a beaver buddy!

Chariot Books™ is an imprint of Chariot Family Publishing
Cook Communications, Colorado Springs, CO 80918
Cook Communications, Paris, Ontario
Kingsway Communications, Eastbourne, England

BARTHOLOMEW BEAVER AND THE STUPENDOUS SPLASH
© 1996 by Michael Waite for text and Sheila Lucas for illustrations

Cover design by Michael Waite
Cover illustration by Sheila Lucas
First printing, 1996
Printed in Canada

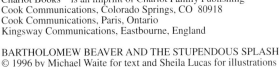